P9-BZU-819

Story play ™

This book belongs to

_____.

This book was read by

_____

on

_____.

Are you ready to start reading the **StoryPlay** way?

Read the story on its own. Play the activities together
as you read!

Ready. Set. Smart!

Text copyright © 2017 by Kate Dopirak
Illustrations copyright © 2017 by Cori Doerrfeld
Prompts and activities © 2017 by Scholastic Inc.

All rights reserved. Published by Scholastic Inc., *Publishers since 1920.* SCHOLASTIC, CARTWHEEL BOOKS, STORYPLAY, and associated logos are trademarks and/or registered trademarks of Scholastic Inc.

Scholastic Inc., 557 Broadway, New York, NY 10012
Scholastic UK Ltd., Euston House, 24 Eversholt Street, London NW1 1DB

No part of this publication may be reproduced, stored in a retrieval system, or transmitted in any form or by any means, electronic, mechanical, photocopying, recording, or otherwise, without written permission of the publisher.
For information regarding permission, write to Scholastic Inc., Attention: Permissions Department, 557 Broadway, New York, NY 10012.

This book is a work of fiction. Names, characters, places, and incidents are either the product of the author's imagination or are used fictitiously, and any resemblance to actual persons, living or dead, business establishments, events, or locales is entirely coincidental.

Library of Congress Cataloging-in-Publication Data available

ISBN 978-0-545-81536-9
10 9 8 7 6 5 4 3 2 1   17 18 19 20 21

Printed in Panyu, China   137
First edition, January 2017
Book design by Doan Buu

Snuggle Bunny

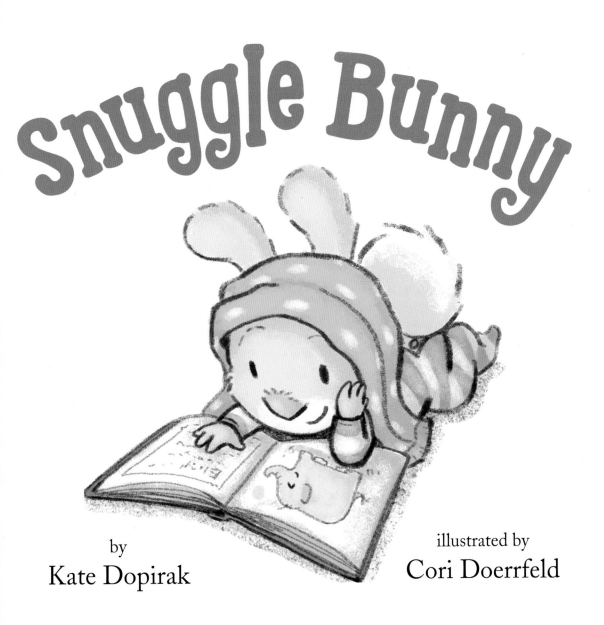

by
Kate Dopirak

illustrated by
Cori Doerrfeld

Cartwheel Books
An Imprint of Scholastic Inc.

For my snuggle bunnies: Josh, Joey, Bobby, and Frankie
– K.D.

For my snuggle kitty: Leo
– C.D.

Wakey, wakey, sleepyhead.
Snuggle Bunny hides in bed.

Blanky, teddy, big-kid cup —

Snuggle Bunny loves his teddy. Do you have a special bedtime buddy?

Snuggle Bunny won't get up!

Mama knows just what to do —
She's a snuggle bunny, too!

What's your favorite song?

Music and a storybook —
Daddy comes to take a look.

Daddy knows just what to do —
He's a snuggle bunny, too!

Building forts and hide-and-seek,

Now that Brother is here, how many bunnies are in this family?

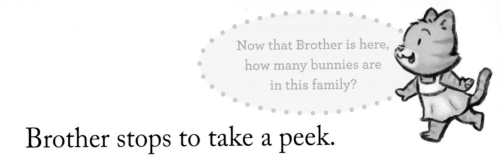

Brother stops to take a peek.

Snuggle Bunny
jumps to say,

"HAPPY
SNUGGLE BUNNY
DAY!"

Does the Bear family have MORE members in it or FEWER members in it than the Fox family?

News spreads out all over town.
Friends line up to snuggle down.

Neighbors all know what to do —
They are snuggle bunnies, too!

More and more from far and wide
Hear the fun and come inside.

Everyone knows what to do —
They are snuggle bunnies, too!

Who is the BIGGEST animal?
Who is the SMALLEST?
Point to them!

Uh-oh!

Big-kid cup falls to the ground,
Makes a rumbly, tumbly sound.

All the floorboards bend and shake.
One by one they start to break . . .

What do you think will happen next?

Creak and crack and crash and boom!
Fall into the dining room!

Snuggle Bunny shouts, "Hooray!"

Breakfast is in bed today.

Story time fun never ends with these creative activities!

★ Fort Fun! ★

Snuggle Bunny, Brother, Mommy, and Daddy build a fort together to play inside. Now it's your turn! Ask an adult to help you build your own fort with these easy tips:

1. Place four chairs in a square shape. Make sure the square is big enough for at least two people to sit down inside, but not too big.
2. Get two big sheets or blankets. Drape one sheet from one chair across the square onto the chair on the opposite side of the square, so the sheet becomes the ceiling of your fort. Drape the other sheet in the same way over the other two chairs.
3. Choose your fort's entrance, and make sure the sheets can open and close for you to come and go.
4. Decorate your fort! You can put a sign on the door, hang stars from the ceiling, or put blankets on the floor and bring pillows inside to make it cozy. It's your fort — have fun!

★ Create Your Own Holiday! ★

Snuggle Bunny made up his own special day — Snuggle Bunny Day! Have you ever wanted to make up YOUR own holiday? Now's your chance!

My day is . . .
This day is in honor of . . .
On this day, we celebrate by . . .
I made up a song for my day. It goes like this . . .